999 Tadpoles
Find a New Home

Written by Ken Kimura
Illustrated by Yasunari Murakami

GECKO PRESS

In spring, Mother Frog laid nine hundred and ninety-nine eggs in the little pond.

One warm day, out hatched nine hundred and ninety-nine tadpoles.

They were tiny, and full of beans.

Mother and Father Frog were delighted.

They told their babies, 'Grow big. Grow strong.'

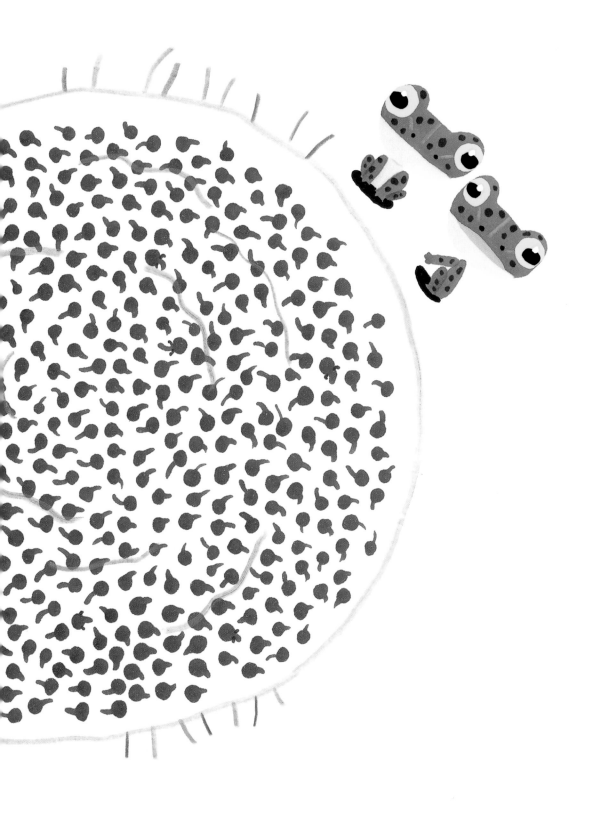

The nine hundred and ninety-nine
tadpoles grew and grew.

All squeezed together in the pond,
they croaked up quite a din.

'Can't move!'

'Can't breathe!'

Mother and Father sighed.

'It's good they've grown but —'

'— what shall we do?'

Both said at the same time:
'We'll have to move.'

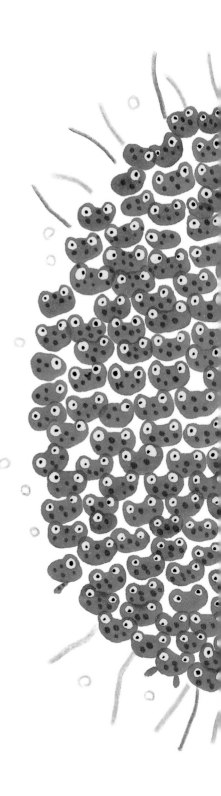

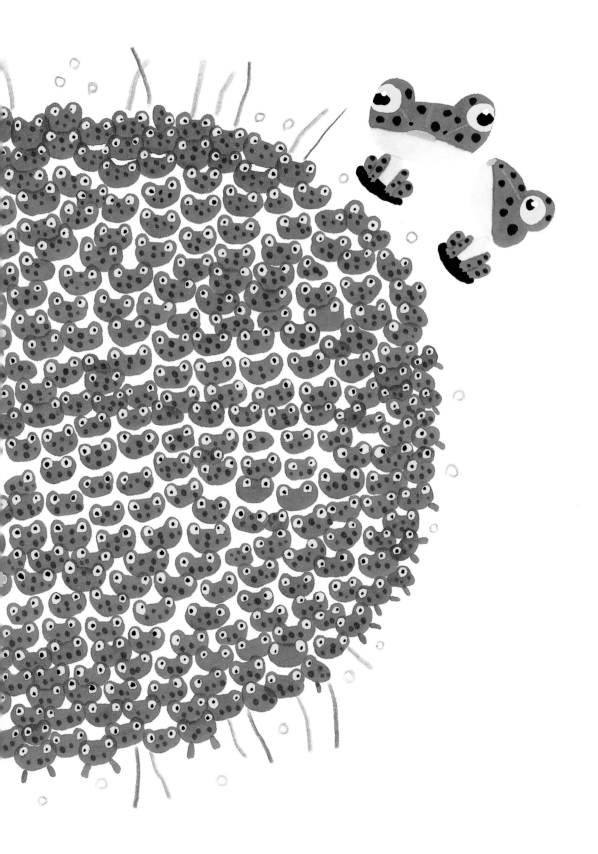

'Cool!'

'We're moving!'

'A new place!'

Nine hundred and ninety-nine excited
little frogs leaped up and down —
up out of the pond.

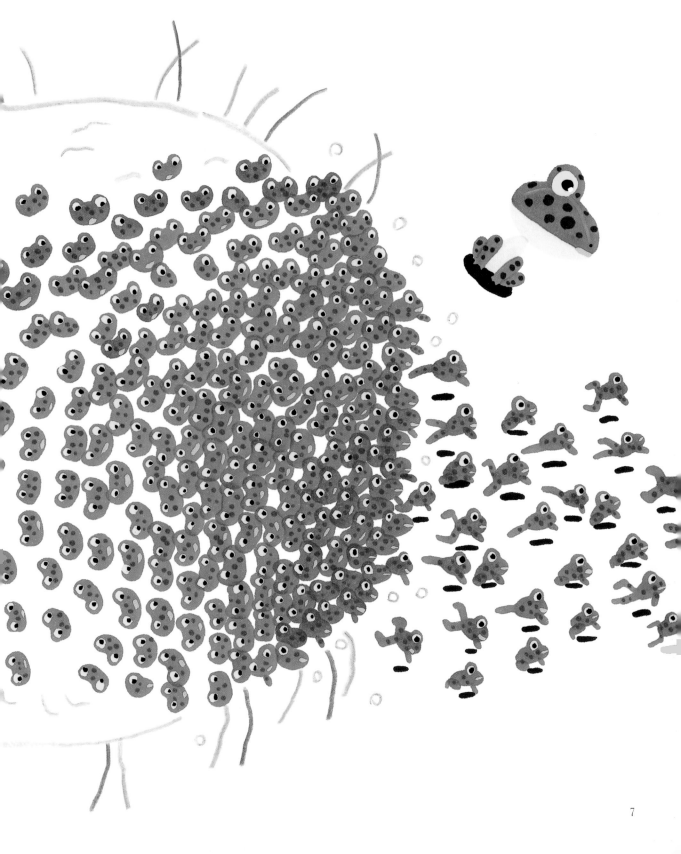

'Be quiet!' said Mother Frog. 'It's a dangerous world out here. We have to be careful. All of you, form a nice long line and follow your father.'

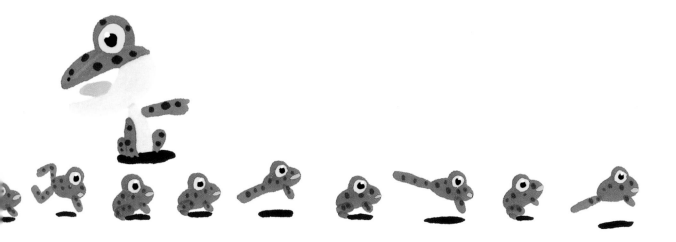

The nine hundred and ninety-nine little
frogs made a long line across the field.

They hopped and hopped, but all they
could see was grass.

The frogs grew tired of the view.

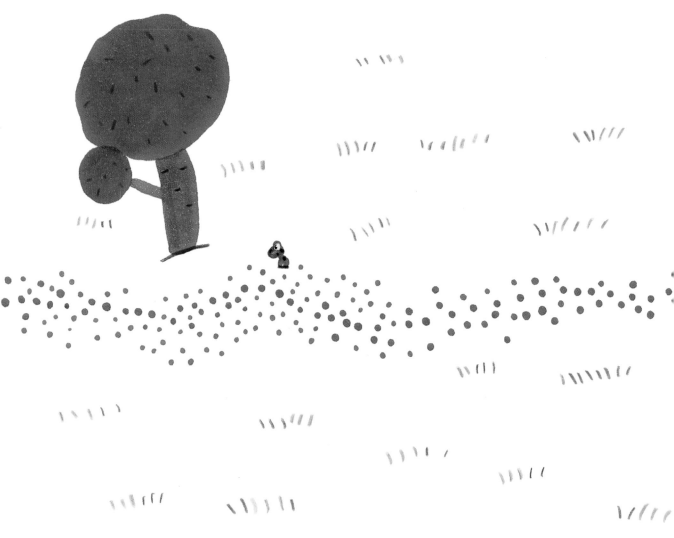

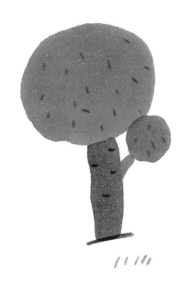

'Are we there yet?'

'Hungry!'

'Sick of hopping.'

'Thirsty.'

'I'm tired!'

'Need water.'

Father Frog warned his children: 'You must keep hopping. Dawdling frogs get snatched by snakes.'

'Snakes?'

'What's a snake?'

'A snake has a very long body and a very wide mouth. It can eat a frog in a single swallow.'

Father Frog shivered.

Five minutes later, hundreds of over-excited frogs were dragging something through the grass.

'Hey, Dad, look what we've found!'

'Is a snake as long as this?'

The thing they were dragging was a mile long.

Mother Frog and Father Frog went pale green.

It was a snake.

It was fast asleep.

Father Frog croaked at the top of his voice,
'All of you, get hopping! Fast as you can!
Quick, before it wakes!'

But just as the nine hundred and ninety-nine little
frogs hopped helter-skelter away from the snake,
the sky darkened. A hungry hawk swooped down.

'Lots of tasty froglets!' he whooped with a grin and…

…snatched up Father Frog in his talons.

Father Frog twisted and struggled as he left the ground.

'No!' he shrieked. 'Let go of me! Let goooo!'

'Hey, pesky frog, keep still!'
The hawk could hardly get
airborne.

'You let my man go!' Mother Frog croaked,
leaping for Father Frog's leg.

'Mum!'

'Wait!'

'Don't leave us!'

The nine hundred and ninety-nine
little frogs leaped after their mother…

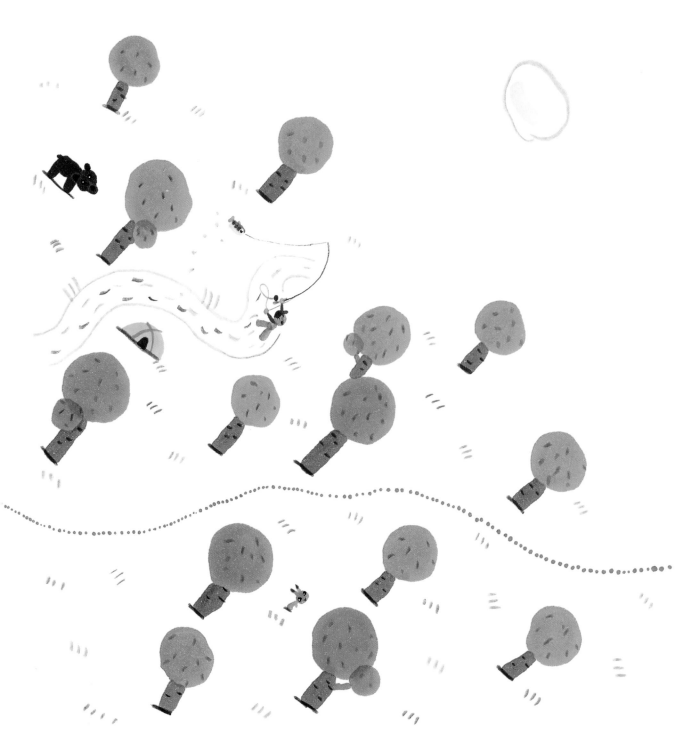

The hawk didn't understand.
How could one frog weigh so much?

Glancing back, he saw a long line of
froglets trailing out behind.

A year's worth of frog feasts!

He was so pleased, he flapped harder.
Up and up he flew.

'Wheee!'

'Look how high we are!'

'This is fantastic!'

The nine hundred and ninety-nine
little frogs were excited.

Mother and Father Frog were worried.

They called down the line: 'Hang on!
Don't let go!'

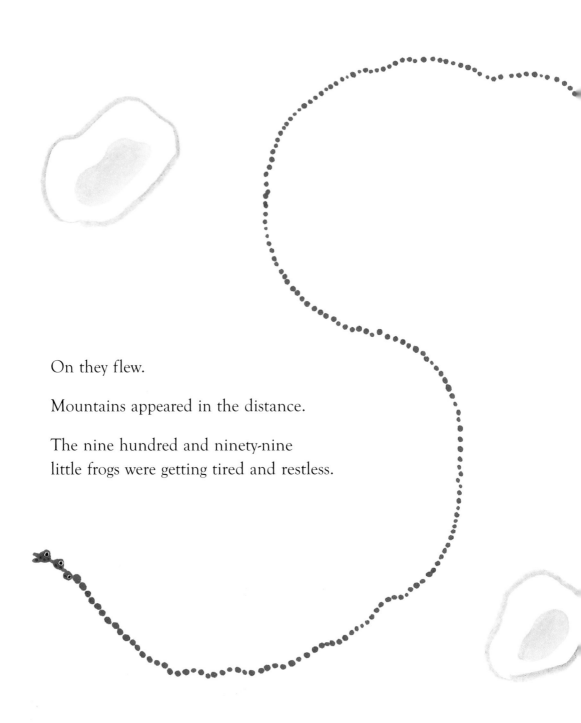

On they flew.

Mountains appeared in the distance.

The nine hundred and ninety-nine
little frogs were getting tired and restless.

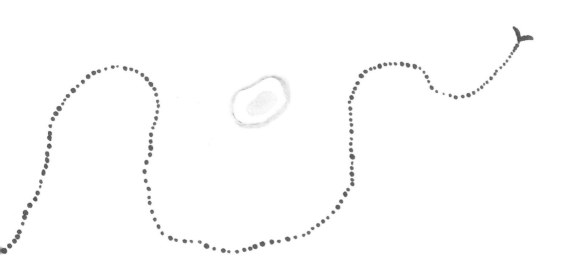

'Where are we going?'

'I'm starving.'

'I want water.'

'Sick of this.'

Whenever the little frogs wriggled or croaked,
the hawk teetered this way and that.

It looked as if he might drop them.

Father Frog begged over and over, 'Please,
Mr Hawk, don't let go. Hang on, please!'

But the hawk couldn't hang on any more.

'I can't...'

...and he dropped them.

'Aaaaaaaargh!'

Father Frog, Mother Frog and nine hundred and ninety-nine little frogs fell...

and fell...

and fell...

Plop!   Plop!   Plop!

Plop!   Plop!

Father Frog, Mother Frog and nine
hundred and ninety-nine little frogs
landed in water.

'Where are we?'

'Must be a big pond.'

The nine hundred and ninety-nine
little frogs were wide-eyed.

'This is big!'

'Nice water!'

'It's huge!'

The nine hundred and ninety-nine
little frogs began to play.

'It's nice here, isn't it?' said Father Frog.

'It's lovely,' said Mother Frog. 'It's big enough for everyone, even when they grow.'

Father croaked for all to hear: 'We're home!'

And this is the end of the story.

The nine hundred and ninety-nine
happy frogs began to chirp:

'Read-it, read-it, read-it, read-it...'

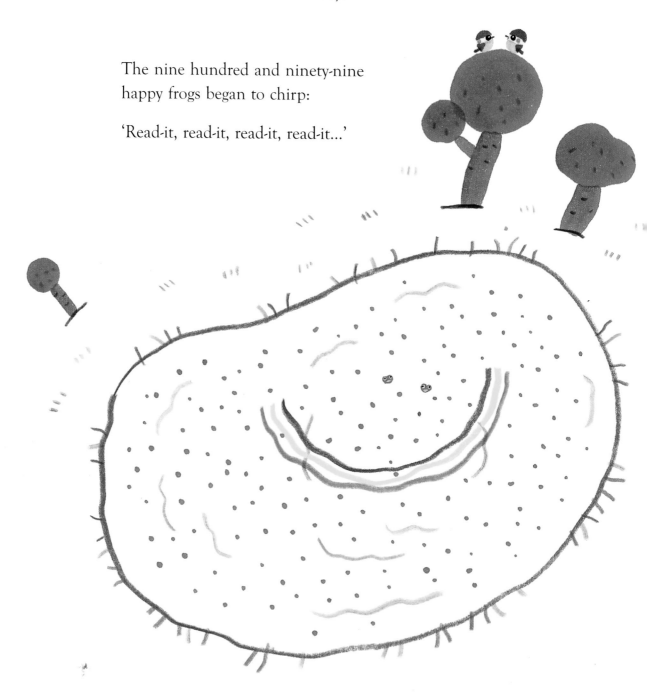